ORCUS on 34th LEVEL

Author: Jon Hook
Project Manager: Edwin Nagy
Editor: Jeff Harkness
Swords & Wizardry Conversion: Jeff Harkness
Art Director: Casey W. Christofferson
Cover Design: Jim Wampler
Front Cover Art: Adrian Landeros
Interior Art: Adrian Landeros, Faith Burgar
Layout: Suzy Moseby
Cartography: Dyson Logos

Frog God Games is:

Bill Webb, Matt Finch, Zach Glazar, Charles A. Wright, Edwin Nagy, Mike Badolato and John Barnhouse

ADVENTURES WORTH WINNING

ISBN: 978-1-6656-0079-8
SW PoD Softcover

Table of Contents

I want to thank the amazing and prolific cartographer, Dyson Logos, for the gift of his "The Lost Temple of Aphosh the Haunted" map. This map, and many more like it, are generously available for free from his website, DysonLogos.com. I made some very slight modifications to Dyson's original map, renamed it "The Candy Crypt", and used it in this adventure. If you enjoy Dyson's maps as much as I do, please consider supporting him by joining his Patreon.

I also want to thank the amazing James M. Spahn for creating such a wonderful toy in the Orcus' Claws and the Crueltide Elves. They were so much fun to play with; I hope my joy is felt by all who read or play this adventure. And finally, I want to say "thank you" to Edwin Nagy for inviting me to write this fun adventure. I was instantly captivated by this idea and it consumed for the twenty days it took me to write it. I was a man possessed by the raging and blood-drenched holiday spirit that oozes from Orcus' Claws. I am forever a changed man — somebody help me, please.

Enjoy!

—Jon Hook

Orcus on 34th Level

By Jon Hook

A Swords & Wizardry adventure for 4 to 6 adventurers of 7th to 9th level

Orcus on 34th Level is a self-contained dungeon crawl adventure for 4–6 adventurers of 7th to 9th level. Recently, the adventurers heard a rumor that jolly ol' Orcus' Claws is preparing to free his wife, Nohell Claws, from a remote dimension where she has been trapped for a thousand years. The ritual can be performed only when the constellation of Gorgon Major is in ascension and the Northern Azure Star shines over the village of Newville. That time is nigh, and if the adventurers fail to stop the ritual, then all *Nohell* is going to break loose!

Beginning the Adventure

For centuries, Orcus' Claws has pined for his one true soul-be-damned mate, a succubus known as Nohell. She is trapped in a null dimension, powerless to affect her own escape, spending a millennium in solitude. But now, as the time of her return draws near, Orcus' Claws has returned to the Candy Crypt, his lair deep within Mount Strumpet. While Orcus' Claws, his Crueltide elves, and the Naughty prepare the candy factory, Mr. Giggles, Claws' demonic astrologer, is conducting the summoning ritual.

The Candy Crypt is intended to be the 34th level of a mega-dungeon; insert it into any dungeon or run it as an isolated subterranean location. The adventurers either stumble upon the Candy Crypt by accident or they may be sent there to thwart Nohell's return. If the local noble hired them, they are promised a reward of 100 gp each. Additionally, each spellcaster will receive a scroll containing three rare spells, while everyone else is promised a master crafted weapon.

As the adventurers descend the spiral staircase that leads to **Room 1**, they hear music echoing through crypt. You are encouraged to play the instrumental song *Christmas Eve Sarajevo* by the Trans-Siberian Orchestra as the game is played. The author wrote lyrics for the song that can be heard echoing through the crypt as well. About one minute after the song begins, and just as the orchestra begins to swell, sing the following lyrics:

> As he flew over the countryside
>
> He listened for your cries,
>
> When from a little village below
>
> He heard the screams arise,
>
> And there he dove to drink in the sight
>
> And bathed in the blood of so many lives!

The Candy Crypt

General Hallways

Unless they are otherwise described, the constructed hallways within the Candy Crypt are 10 feet wide and 12 feet high. The walls and ceiling are expertly crafted stone and mortar; the floors are mortared cobblestone. Wall sconces with lit torches are spaced every 40 feet. If no specific decorations are described, the walls and ceiling have a color like pale sand, but the cobblestones used in the floor are a multitude of hues in rose, amber, umber, and chocolate.

Room 1: Window Shopping

Your boots clang on the wrought-iron stairs as you spiral your way down to the floor. It's difficult to gauge the depth of the room, because every surface is covered in mirrors: the floor, the walls, the ceiling, the doors, and the columns. Four torches illuminate this room; each torch is seated in an iron sconce mounted in the corners of the room. Three columns hold up the room's ceiling, while the fourth column is shattered on the floor. The door on the north wall is slightly ajar.

The characters see an amazing sight as they enter this room, as their reflections repeat to infinity in every direction. Every character must make a saving throw to avoid being confused by the infinite reflections. On a failed save, the character suffers a –2 penalty on all dice rolls while in this room.

Three reflection ghosts are trapped within this room, one inside each column. A fourth ghost used to be in the room, but one of the columns was destroyed, releasing the ghost and allowing it to escape. Each column is also linked to one of the room's four doors; if anyone whispers the secret name of the ghost tied to that particular door, it opens. If a ghost escapes the room, the associated door is permanently unlocked. While locked, nothing — no spell or blade — can harm or unlock the door.

THE CANDY CRYPT
1 Square - 5 Feet
Thanks to Dyson Logos
for the original map
1
2
3
4
5
6
7
8
9
10
11
12
X 13 X   X
14
15
16
17
X
18
19

Reflection ghosts are invisible, immaterial, and intangible; they cannot be harmed, nor can they harm anyone as a ghost. However, a reflection ghost can manifest as a mirror image opposite any character that touches any reflective surface (walking does not count as touching a surface). Up to three mirrored manifestations can appear in this room, one from each intact column. A manifested reflection steps out of the mirror to battle its counterpart, fully equipped with all the character's gear and abilities, including hit points. If the mirror manifestation is destroyed, the reflection ghost returns to its column, until it manifests again.

Each column has 25 hit points and is linked to a different doorway. If a column is destroyed, it also unlocks the connected doorway. The southwest column is linked to the door on the west wall, the northeast column to the door on the east wall, and the southeast column to the door on the south wall. The shattered northwest column was linked to the door on the north wall; that door unlocked when the column was destroyed. Unfortunately, destroying the columns also weakens the structural integrity of the chamber. The ceiling has a 20% cumulative chance of collapsing during any intense fighting for each column that is destroyed; if all three remaining columns are destroyed, there's an 80% chance of collapse (don't forget the 20% chance for the already destroyed column). Characters must make a saving throw to escape the room if the ceiling collapses. On a failed save, the character takes 2d6 points of damage from falling stones and shards of mirror.

If the characters don't touch any reflective surfaces, it is possible for them to exit the room through the unlocked door in the north wall without manifesting any of the trapped reflection ghosts.

Room 2: Christmas Wishing Well

It is difficult to see the ceiling in this hallway; it's at least 30 feet high. Hundreds of iron chains ending with hooks dangle from the shadows. They slowly sway and jingle like bells as they clink against each other. Most of the hooks hang seven to eight feet off the floor. At the far end of the hall, a column of light illuminates a fountain of showering water.

This long hallway features two large niches near **Room 1**. Each niche is filled with chains dangling from the ceiling, with 3d4 corpses hanging from the hooks. The corpses are soft and wet, but instead of smelling like death, each one smells like strawberries, sugarplums, peaches, and honeysuckle. Each corpse is dressed in tattered undergarments; none of the corpses has any treasure.

The hallway features an eastward branch that caved in. Rubble completely blocks the passage, with 15 feet of debris separating this hallway from **Room 9**. Dwarven characters can easily assess the rubble and see that with enough time it is possible to clear the way. It takes 10 hours for a single dwarf to dig through the rubble; divide the time by the number of dwarves to determine how long it takes to clear the branch. Any two non-dwarf characters equal one dwarf when it comes to the task of digging.

An eerie beam of light shines down from the ceiling directly over the fountain at the far northern end of the hallway. The marbled fountain has two basins: a small basin on a slim pedestal standing over a larger basin. Water cascades out of the upper basin and falls into the lower basin. A marble sculpture of crossed and bloodied candy canes stands upright in the center of the upper basin. The lower basin is lined with jagged, rusty nails, and its edge is stained dark brown with old blood. Swimming around inside the lower basin are small spheres of light that cast a dull yellow glow. The tiny balls of light move like goldfish.

The little glowing balls of light are nearly impossible to catch. The only way to catch a ball of light is for characters to stab their hands on the rusty nails, taking 1d4 points of damage, and then plunge their bleeding hands into the water. If this is done, a glowing ball swims directly into the open wound and buries itself in the character's flesh. The glowing ball is absorbed, and the character must make a saving throw with a –4 penalty. Nothing happens on a successful save. If a character fails the saving throw, however, his or her alignment changes to Chaotic. If the character's alignment is already Chaotic, he or she is granted one wish (as per a *wish* spell). Any single Chaotic character may receive only one wish, and any attempt to gain a second results in 3d6 hooked chains grabbing the character and dealing 1d6 points of damage per hook. The character's body is lifted up and pulled into one of the niches near **Room 1**. The character's corpse is stored until it can be processed into candy.

Room 3: Dead Letter Office

The door to this chamber easily swings open. A rustling sound from beyond reminds you of the wind blowing through the trees. A large creature that looks more like a plant with four long and twisted tentacled limbs sits behind a desk covered in papers. The strange creature holds a quill curled within each appendage as it writes four letters simultaneously.

The creature's vegetable flesh appears long and rubbery; it is covered in leaves, thorns, and clusters of bright red berries. It stares at you from two hollow, coal-black eyes. Its wide toothy maw splits open as it yells, "I'm not ready yet!" The creature flips the desk and charges!

The creature is a **mistletroll**. Its job is to write threatening letters to children promising that Orcus' Claws will sneak into their homes and steal them away from their parents to convert them into the Naughty so they can serve in Claws' Candy Crypt for all eternity. If the characters search the mistletroll's desk, they discover a small chest with 3d10 gp.

Mistletroll: HD 7; **HP** 38; **AC** 4[15]; **Atk** 4 thorny vines (1d4 + envelop), bite (1d8); **Move** 12; **Save** 11; **AL** C; **CL/XP** 9/1100; **Special:** envelop (save or entangle, Open Doors check to break free), regenerate (3 hp/round), poison berries (save or die, 2d10 damage and sick [–1 to hit and saves for 1 hour] with successful save), spore breath weapon (1/day, 20ft cloud, save or die in 1d4 weeks as new mistletroll grows in host, 2d6 damage on successful save and sick for 2d6 rounds [–1 to hit]), vulnerable to fire (200%). **(Appendix A: New Monsters)**

Room 4: Hot from the Oven

As soon as the door opens, you are greeted by the welcoming smell of warm bread baking. Most of the room is filled with low metal tables covered in flour. A life-sized statue of Orcus' Claws holding a reindeer's severed head stands on a short dais near the south wall, and a large clay oven dominates the north wall. The room is a beehive of activity by almost two dozen small gingersnap men. The cookie-men ignore you because they are intensely focused on their task of making more gingersnap men.

When the characters enter this room, 20 gingersnap men are busy making more cookie-men. Ten gingersnap men are working at the metal tables as they shape raw ginger cookie dough into new cookie-men; five gingersnap men are stirring a large bowl of raw cookie dough batter together in the northeast corner, and five gingersnap men are working in front of the oven. The oven workers insert raw, lifeless cookie-men and extract brand-new, fully baked and animated gingersnap men.

The clay oven is fueled by hellfire. Any non-gingersnap man that enters the oven takes 10d10 points of damage each round (or half damage with a successful saving throw). Five new gingersnap men exit the oven every third combat round, even if they must crawl out on their own. The gingersnap men ignore the characters as long as they do not attempt to leave this room through the door that leads to the cavernous areas of **Rooms 5, 6, and 7**, and as long as they do not interfere with their baking operation. The oven has a pair of metal doors that can be closed over the fiery opening. If the oven doors are closed and magically locked (by casting *hold portal* or *wizard lock*), the oven fires are snuffed out in 2d6 rounds.

The statue of Orcus' Claws has a pair of precious rubies for eyes. Each ruby is worth 150 gp. The statue is magically trapped. If anyone touches either ruby eye, that person is teleported into the oven. *Detect magic* informs the spellcaster that the ruby eyes are magically trapped, but does not reveal the exact nature of the trap. *Dispel magic* successfully disarms the trap for 10 minutes (divide the caster's level by nine to calculate the percentage chance of success). The trap was originally cast by Orcus' Claws' astrologer, Mr. Giggles.

Gingersnap Men (20+): HD: 4; **HP** 20 each; **AC** 5[14]; **Atk** weapon (1d4); **Move** 14; **Save** 13; **AL** C; **CL/XP** 7/600; **Special:** immune to fire and mind control, vulnerable to water (200%). **(Appendix A: New Monsters)**

The temperature drops dramatically as you enter this cavernous area, causing your breath to exhale as a cloud of warm vapor. The walls and floors sparkle with ice crystals, and the entire cavern is composed of ice cream. You see a quarry pit filled with gingersnap men toiling away as they excavate chunks of chocolate ore and veins of caramel from the ice cream walls. Flying over the gingersnap men, directing their work, is a trio of large demonic-looking snowy owls.

The gingersnap men baked in **Room 4** are sent to the ice cream quarry to work. Gingersnap men are a mindless race; it is thus impossible for the characters to stoke a rebellion in them. When the adventurers enter, 15 gingersnap men are working in the quarry. The gingersnap men ignore the characters; they attack only if their work is interrupted. On the other hand, the demonic owls, also known as kringkuks, attack the adventurers on sight. The kringkuks have a quota of ore to collect, and they will not allow the characters to threaten their work schedule.

The gingersnap men collect ore and place it in carts that are wheeled to **Room 7** for processing. One of the carts currently parked in an alcove along the eastern wall of the cavern contains some other ore the gingersnap men discovered, including 3d20 ingots of gold "*sprinkles.*" Each ingot is worth 10 gp. An intelligent dagger named *Frost Fang* is also in the cart; the blade was unable to communicate with the mindless gingersnap men (see **Appendix B: New Magic Items**). The gingersnap men also found a large magical gem known as an *ice storm sapphire* worth 500 gp that can cast *ice storm* (see **Appendix B: New Magic Items**).

Gingersnap Men (15): HD: 4; **HP** 20 each; **AC** 5[14]; **Atk** weapon (1d4); **Move** 14; **Save** 13; **AL** C; **CL/XP** 7/600; **Special:** immune to fire and mind control, vulnerable to water (200%). **(Appendix A: New Monsters)**

Kringkuk Demons (3): HD 6; **HP** 39, 34, 32; **AC** 1[18]; **Atk** 2 talons (1d6), bite (1d8 + poison venom); **Move** 6 (fly 16); **Save** 11; **AL** C; **CL/XP** 10/1400; **Special:** immune to cold, poison venom (2d4 damage, save for half damage), resistances (electricity, fire, poison) (50%), webbing (3/day, 20ft cube, as *web* spell). **(Appendix A: New Monsters)**

ICE CREAM CAVES

The Ice Cream Caves are extremely cold. The characters must make a saving throw for every half hour they spend in the frozen caves. On a failed save, the character takes 1d4 points of damage from the cold.

ROOM 6: CHOCOLATE FALLS

The cavern's ceiling here is 60 feet high. From high above, a fountain of chocolate spews out and falls into a pool of chocolate below. Several large chunks of dark chocolate fudge float in the pool of light-brown milk chocolate.

None of the gingersnap men works near the chocolate pool. Several large boulder-like scoops of ice cream near the pool provide cover for the characters if they choose to hide near the pool. Characters who drink the liquid chocolate satiate their hunger for a full day. If the characters spend more than five minutes near the pool's edge, the **chocolate pudding** emerges and attacks.

Chocolate Pudding: HD 6; **HP** 30; **AC** 8[11]; **Atk** smother (2d6); **Move** 6; **Save** 11; **AL** N; **CL/XP** 7/600; **Special:** +1 or better magic weapons to hit, vulnerable to water (1d6 damage per round). **(Appendix A: New Monsters)**

The gingersnap men push carts of candied ore to a basket at the base of the cliff wall below the processing station. The gingersnap men transfer the ore from the cart to the basket, which is then pulled up to the processing station by Crueltide elves. The elves unload the basket, sort the ore, and load it onto conveyer belts that carry the ore through a small tunnel in the eastern wall.

Eight Crueltide elves sing the haunting carol the adventurers first heard as they descended into **Room 1**. The elves are sorting the ore mined by the gingersnap men into different piles. The ore is loaded onto a conveyer belt system that runs through small tunnels dug through the east wall to deliver the ore to the Bittersweet Treats chamber (**Room 14**).

The conveyer belt tunnel is exceedingly small; only a creature of halfling size or smaller can fit through the tunnel. The tunnel is incredibly claustrophobic, and anyone attempting to travel through the conveyer belt tunnel must make a saving throw every 30 feet or take 1 hit point of damage from asphyxiation.

The Crueltide elves are focused on their work and most likely do not notice the characters until they enter their work area. Each Crueltide elf carries 1d2 items from the **Crueltide Contraptions Chart** within a *bag of limited holding* (see **Appendix B: New Magic Items**), a pocketful of 2d6 miniature candy canes, and a dagger.

Crueltide Elves (8): HD 2; **HP** 16, 14x2, 13, 11x2, 10, 9; **AC** 7[12]; **Atk** dagger (1d4) or deadly contraption; **Move** 12; **Save** 16; **AL** C; **CL/XP** 3/60; **Special:** Crueltide contraptions (deadly toys), darkvision (60ft). **(Appendix A: New Monsters)**

Equipment: dagger, *bag of limited holding*, 2d6 miniature candy canes.

ROOM 8: BUBBLEGUM REFUSE

A half dozen shovel-wielding Crueltide elves are working in this room. Several piles of broken toys, pieces of warped candy, crumbled cookies, and other heaping piles of junk are scattered about the room. The demonic elves are shoveling the debris into a sunken area in the northwest corner of the room where a large pink sphere is located in the lower section of the room. The rubbery-looking sphere warbles as the junk the elves keep shoveling penetrates its elastic skin.

This is the disposal room. Anything broken or no longer useful is chucked into the bubblegum sphere for the creature to consume. Each Crueltide elf in this room carries a shovel, a dagger, and a small *bag of limited holding* (see **Appendix B: New Magic Items**) containing 1d2 Crueltide contraptions (see **Crueltide Contraptions Table**). Many precious items were discarded by mistake; each character who searches through the piles of refuse may roll once on the **Random Treasure Table** below. Each treasure can be found only once; reroll all duplicate results.

The large pink bubblegum sphere is ravenous and must be continually fed by the Crueltide elves. If the feeding ceases, the bubblegum sphere lifts off from the dais it is sitting on and floats into the room to attack anyone threatening its constant food supply.

Bubblegum Sphere: HD 5; **HP** 32; **AC** 8[11]; **Atk** strike (paralysis + glue); **Move** 6 (flying); **Save** 12; **AL** N; **CL/XP** 6/400; **Special:** digest (2d4 damage per round to stuck targets), glue (target stuck after successful strike, save avoids), immune to lightning and fire, paralysis (save avoids). **(Appendix A: New Monsters)**

Crueltide Elves (6): HD 2; **HP** 13, 12x2, 10, 9x2; **AC** 7[12]; **Atk** dagger (1d4) or shovel (1d6) or deadly contraption; **Move** 12; **Save** 16; **AL** C; **CL/XP** 3/60; **Special:** Crueltide contraptions (deadly toys), darkvision (60ft). **(Appendix A: New Monsters)**

Equipment: dagger, shovel, *bag of limited holding*.

1d12	Result
1	A small sack with 3d10 gold coins.
2	A quiver with 2d4 arrows. Each arrowhead glows a soft green. Each enchanted arrow bestows a +2 to hit and inflicts 1d6 + 2 points of damage, but this quiver is in the junkpile for a reason: The arrows are unstable. Each time one of these arrows is nocked and drawn, roll 1d6: On a 1, the arrow explodes in the archer's hands and inflicts 1d6 + 2 points of damage to the archer and destroys the bow.
3	A small sack with 2d3 tiny gemstones (diamonds, emeralds, rubies, and sapphires); each gem is worth 50 gp.
4	A small figurine of a silver eagle. The figurine transforms into an eagle when the command word is spoken and is capable of hunting or fighting for its master. If slain, it transforms back into a figurine and may be used again. The figurine may be used only once per week. **Eagle: HD** 1; **HP** 7; **AC** 8[11]; **Atk** 2 talons (1d3), bite (1d4+1); **Move** 3/24 (flying); **Save** 17; **AL** N; **CL/XP** 2/30; **Special:** none.
5	A small locked box from which leaks thin tendrils of vapor that have an acrid, electrical smell. The lock is not trapped, but the object inside — a large diamond containing an enchanted lightning bolt — is unstable. If the box is opened, the lightning bolt automatically discharges, striking everyone within 10 feet for 3d6 points of damage, or half damage with a successful saving throw. Once the lightning bolt discharges, the diamond is no longer enchanted but is still worth 600 gp.
6	A small sack with 2d12 gold coins and a golden ring etched with an image of a skeleton. It is a *ring of X-ray vision* worth 150 gp.
7	A filthy and stained burlap sack that stinks of rot and decay. Inside is a thick skeletal left hand covered in moldy, green-gray flesh. Each of the four fingers stands up and erect, and the thumb is tucked in close to the palm. Each of the four fingertips has a small black wick showing. Each finger of the hand of glory is enchanted with a spell that activates when that finger's candlewick is lit: index, *sleep*; middle, *knock;* ring, *hold person*; and pinky, *fear*. Each finger candle can be lit only three times, after which the finger curls over the thumb. The hand contains a vile and corrupt intelligence that telepathically whispers to whoever possesses it.
8	A shabby, floppy purple hat with two white feathers. Any character who puts on the hat must make a saving throw or permanently lose 1 point of charisma. With a successful save, the adventurer intuitively knows how to play any musical instrument and the lyrics to every known adventure ballad. While the adventurer is wearing the hat and entertaining with music and song, everyone within a 20-foot radius gains a +1 to attacks and saving throws.
9	A small velvet sack containing 2d10 enchanted six-sided dice that radiate warmth and have a soft green glow. The character can roll any number of the six-sided dice simultaneously. For each die, consult the table below. After a die is rolled, that die dissolves into smoke and is lost forever.

1	Permanently lose 1 point of constitution
2	Lose 1 hit point
3	1d3 gemstones worth 80 gp each appear in the character's pocket
4	Gain 1 temporary point of strength (vanishes in 12 hours)
5	A single black rose appears; touching it grants the character 100 XP but the rose then withers and dies
6	Gain 1 hit point (any hit points gained above the character's current maximum are temporary and vanish in 1d6 hours)

1d12	Result
10	A small sack appears with 6d6 tiny gemstones (diamond, emeralds, rubies, and sapphires), each worth 20 gp.
11	A hollowed-out ram's horn fashioned into a war horn. When sounded, everyone within a 60-foot radius of the horn must make a saving throw. On a successful save, the affected individual gains a battle fury that grants a +2 to-hit bonus and a +1 AC bonus. On a failed save, the affected individual gains an uncontrollable blood lust that grants a +2 to-hit bonus and a –1 AC penalty, and they must attack the closest individual (friend or foe). The effects last for 2d3 rounds.
12	A coal-black warhammer appears. This dark weapon is enchanted with the soul of a demon named Cruuf'xk. The evil weapon tempts its wielder to crush the skulls of everyone around it (see **Appendix B: New Magic Items**).

Room 9: Contraption Factory

From the hallway outside, it is easy to hear the *ting-ting* of tiny hammers crafting deadly toys. Inside the room, it is dark and poorly lit. Working in the room are 10 Crueltide elves, each seated at a table with a pair of low-burning candles providing the lighting needed for their tasks. The room is old — ancient even — and the ceiling sags, a portion of the north wall has fallen in, and a corridor to the west has collapsed and is full of rubble.

The Crueltide elves in this chamber are old; they seem as ancient and feeble as the room itself. None of them has the strength or stamina to battle the adventurers, but several new experimental contraptions are ready to defend their creators: the meka-men! Each meka-man stands seven feet tall and is made of iron. Their bodies are covered in filigree and fancy sculpting details, and they are painted in bright colors with rosy red cheeks and big eyes. Four of the meka-men wield swords, while three hold wands.

Each geriatric Crueltide elf has only 1 hit point and no armor; they are easily slain. Anyone searching the room may roll 1d6: on a 1–4, they find broken and incomplete contraptions; on a 5–6, they find one contraption (roll on the **Crueltide Contraptions Table**).

Elderly Crueltide Elves (10): HD 2; **HP** 1x10; **AC** 9[10]; **Atk** none; **Move** 12; **Save** 16; **AL** C; **CL/XP** 3/60; **Special:** darkvision (60ft). (**Appendix A: New Monsters**)

Note: The characters receive no XP for killing these ancient creatures.

Meka-Man Fighters (4): HD 4; **HP** 25x4; **AC** 2[17]; **Atk** sword (1d8) or fist (1d4+1); **Move** 12; **Save** 13; **AL** N; **CL/XP** 6/400; **Special:** none. (**Appendix A: New Monsters**)

Meka-Man Wizards (3): HD 4; **HP** 25x3; **AC** 2[17]; **Atk** wand (2d4) or fist (1d4+1); **Move** 12; **Save** 13; **AL** N; **CL/XP** 6/400; **Special:** none. (**Appendix A: New Monsters**)

Room 10: Lost Souls

The tortured moans and cries of prisoners fill this room. A curtain of chains separates this room from a corridor to the north, and an open sarcophagus positioned above a bed of red-hot coals is along the south wall. Exhausted and defeated prisoners are shackled to the walls. Their torturers are a band of twisted people with horns, demonic grins, hooved feet, and stinger tails. One of them sees your crew of adventurers and says, "Oh look! Fresh meat!"

The demonic creatures are known as the Naughty. This room is where they torture their hapless victims. They place a prisoner into the sarcophagus and then fill it with candy canes. The coals under the sarcophagus are stoked until the candy canes melt. The Naughty then remove the candied golem and place it in **Room 11** for safekeeping. If rescued, the prisoners can help the characters as hirelings fighting for their freedom, and if a character dies, a prisoner can serve as a replacement. The insanity and torture the prisoners endured has turned them all into berserkers; their toughened skin provides an Armor Class akin to leather armor.

The Naughty (13): HD 2; HP 15, 13, 12, 10x3, 9x2, 8x2, 7x3; AC 3[16]; **Atk** barbed whip (1d4+1) or red-hot poker (1d4) or stinger (1d3 + paralysis); **Move** 12; **Save** 16; **AL** C; **CL/XP** 3/60; **Special:** paralysis (1d4 turns, save with −2 penalty avoids). (**Appendix A: New Monsters**) **Equipment:** barbed whip, red-hot poker.

Human, Berserkers (5): HD 1; HP 7x5; AC 7[12]; **Atk** weapon (by weapon) or fist (1d3); **Move** 12; **Save** 17; **AL** N; **CL/XP** 2/30; **Special:** berserk (+2 to hit).

Room 11: Sweet Tomb

This circular chamber has a 25-foot-high domed ceiling and five niches evenly spaced around the northern hemisphere of the room. A large sarcophagus is within each niche. The lid of each sarcophagus is sculpted to resemble a giant candy-jellied bear, and each is painted a different color: blue, red, yellow, green, and purple. A two-foot-diameter red-and-white striped orb hangs from a short chain in the center of the domed ceiling. The orb spins slowly.

As the characters enter this chamber, the spinning orb begins to glow with an internal white light that pulses like a heartbeat. The orb returns to a dormant mode when no one is in the room. Each jelly-bear sarcophagus contains 2d3 + 1 candied golems that the Naughty created in **Room 10**. They are piled in the crypts like cordwood. Each candied golem is in a state of suspended animation; the key to their animation is slowly spinning on the ceiling.

The orb fires a bolt of lightning at two sarcophagi every three combat rounds. When the lightning strikes, one of the candied golems inside each sarcophagus animates. The golems slide open their tombs and lumber out to attack.

The secret to this room is to destroy the spinning orb. Without it, the candied golems cannot be reanimated. Once destroyed, the orb explodes and deals 3d6 points of damage to everyone in the room. However, each time the orb is attacked, it retaliates with a lightning bolt. Any character killed by one of the orb's lightning bolts is reanimated as a zombie on the next combat round.

Candied Golems (2d3+1): HD 8; HP 45; AC 7[12]; **Atk** 2 fists (2d8); **Move** 12; **Save** 8; **AL** N; **CL/XP** 13/2300; **Special:** immune to most spells (affected only by fire-based spells), immune to slashing and piercing weapons. (**Appendix A: New Monsters**)

The Orb: HD 4; HP 30; AC 4[15]; **Atk** lightning bolt (2d10); **Move** 0 (immobile); **AL** N; **CL/XP** 4/120; **Special:** explode (if destroyed, 3d6 damage in 30ft radius, save for half damage), reanimation (animate dead [as zombie] or inanimate objects [candied golems]).

The music heard throughout this candied crypt grows louder as you approach this chamber. As you enter, you discover a 13-piece demonic orchestra, but each humanoid musician is skinless and their instruments are abominations constructed out of bones. Standing on the small stage is the choir, a quartet of demons singing in perfect harmony.

As noted in **Beginning the Adventure** above, remind the players about the music and the singing that echoes through this dungeon. The orchestra is impervious to harm. If a musician is slain, it just stands back up during the next combat round to continue playing its instrument. If its instrument is destroyed, it automatically knits back together so it can be played again. The musicians have no action other than playing music.

The four members of the choir are erinyes demons. At least one erinyes must continue singing to maintain control of the orchestra. The erinyes are not carrying their whips, but they do have their bronze swords. If all four erinyes are destroyed, their grip on the orchestra is released. As soon as the last erinyes dies, the orchestra changes its tune and begins playing a melody that sounds like the opening theme music for the *Tales from the Crypt* television series. The new song also echoes throughout the Candy Crypt. The orchestra's musicians despise Orcus' Claws, so the new song bestows a +1 to-hit bonus and a +1 bonus to saving throws while the new song is playing.

Erinyes Demons (4): HD 6; **HP** 42, 40, 38, 36; **AC** 2[17]; **Atk** bronze sword (1d6 + paralysis); **Move** 12 (fly 24); **Save** 11; **AL** C; **CL/XP** 10/1400; **Special:** fear (appearance causes fear as spell, save resists), immune to fire and cold, magic resistance (25%), paralysis (save avoids), spell-like abilities. (*Monstrosities* 93)

Spell-like abilities: at will—*detect invisibility, locate object.*

The floor and ceiling of this long hallway are painted a bright white. The walls are decorated with brightly painted frescos depicting the mighty Orcus' Claws visiting merry mayhem on hapless villagers.

A new fresco image is found every 10 feet along the hallway. Starting at **Room 1** (fresco 1 on table below) and running to **Room 18** (fresco 10), the images depicted along the hallway are:

Fresco	Description
1	Orcus' Claws driving his sleigh through a pale evening sky filled with black stars.
2	Orcus' Claws looking jolly as his reindeer are slaughtering and eating frightened villagers.
3	Orcus' Claws stuffing frightened children into his bulging sack.
4	Orcus' Claws relaxing and reclining in a comfy chair as he pulls a strip of meat off a bone with his teeth. The foot on the leg is still wearing a pink bunny slipper. Claws has a glass of milk in his other hand. (Trapped)
5	Orcus' Claws looking over his shoulder to smile and wink at the viewer as he warms his hands over a burning holiday tree with a restrained family tied to the trunk.
6	Orcus' Claws placing bloodstained weapons decorated in colorful ribbons and bows under the holiday tree. A severed hand lies nearby in a pool of bright red blood. (Trapped)
7	Orcus' Claws in full belly laugh as a trio of animated dolls with knives surround and menacingly close in on a frightened little girl.
8	Orcus' Claws placing a large candy cane into a stocking nailed to a fireplace mantel, but the stocking is already bulging and overstuffed with creepy crawling insects. A wet eyeball with a few inches of optical nerve sits on the mantel near the stocking. (Trapped)
9	Orcus' Claws walking back toward his sleigh. Two crying and defeated kids are slung over one shoulder, and he drags a third kid behind him by the hair.
10	Orcus' Claws and his sleigh of flying reindeer silhouetted against a full moon as a village burns below them.

The hallway is trapped at Frescos 4, 6, and 8:

Fresco No. 4 Trap: Anyone stepping in front of this fresco must make a saving throw or fall 10 feet into a 20-foot-by-20-foot room. **Three jackals of darkness** with glowing red eyes stalk the room and instantly attack anyone who falls into their den.

Jackals of Darkness (3): HD 4; **HP** 29, 26, 24; **AC** 4[15]; **Atk** bite (1d6); **Move** 14; **Save** 13; **AL** C; **CL/XP** 5/240; **Special:** black fire (creature's aura envelops one chosen creature within 50ft, 1 point of damage per round). (*Monstrosities* 269)

Fresco No. 6 Trap: A huge axe blade swings on a pendulum between the walls to strike at anyone stepping in front of this fresco (attacking as a 6HD creature, 2d8 damage). The frescos conceal the slit from which the pendulum swings, but a successful secret doors check reveals the concealed opening. After the blade swings, dozens of poisoned needles rain down from the ceiling. All creatures in a 10-foot area in front of the fresco must make a saving throw or be struck by 1d4 + 2 poisoned needles. The needles do 1d3 points of damage each, and the creature dies a painful death in 1d6 turns if it fails a saving throw. If the creature succeeds on the saving throw, it still takes 2d6 points of damage from the poison.

Fresco No. 8 Trap: The 10-foot-by-10-foot section of floor in front of this fresco is thin and easily breaks away. Anyone stepping in front of this fresco sinks into a pit filled with insects (centipedes, millipedes, spiders, beetles, cockroaches, worms, etc.). The pit is 30 feet deep, and it's filled nearly to the top with insects. Because of the insects' constant squirming, anyone caught in the pit begins to quickly sink and drown.

Characters must succeed on a saving throw each round to "swim" through the insects and keep their head above the squirming mass. Insect bites inflict 1 point of damage each round to characters who make their saving throw but remain in the pit. Anyone who fails their saving throw submerges and takes 1d6 points of damage each round. They can succeed on a saving throw on the next round to claw their way back to the surface. Characters who fail three saves in a row drown in the insects. Due to their massive numbers, weapons have no effect on the pit full of insects.

Room 14: Bittersweet Treats

This room is a beehive of activity. Raw candy ore is delivered on a series of conveyer belts. The ore is plucked from the belts, torn and crushed into smaller bits, and then mixed with other components to create pounds of tasty holiday treats. Four large tentacled monstrosities are hard at work in this candy factory; each of their tentacles is decorated in little silver bells that jangle as they work. If the legends are to be believed, before you are a quartet of jingle grells!

The jingle grells are focused on their work, and they attack the characters only if they are attacked first or if any character enters their zone. Each jingle grell works in a 20-foot-by-20-foot zone separated by a thick column. At the rear of each zone, a narrow passage leads to the conveyor belt from **Room 7**. Some of the ore is automatically scraped off the belt as it passes each location, making a slowly growing pile for jingle grells to use.

If the jingle grells are defeated, the characters discover stacks and stacks of boxed candied treats and the corpse of an unfortunate soul who lost his life to the jingle grells long ago.

The corpse is that of Montague J. Sebastian, a famed astrologer, sage, and wizard who vanished many years ago. It seems that the characters have solved the riddle of his disappearance. Sebastian's corpse holds the following treasures: *boots of elvenkind*, *cloak of elvenkind*, a *ring of protection +2*, a *staff of power*, an ivory and mahogany *+2 crossbow* with a dozen silver bolts (+2 damage / +4 damage versus undead), a *wand of lightning bolts* (5 charges, 4d6 damage), a small chest with 3d20 + 20 gp and 2d8 precious gems (40 gp each), and his spellbook, which contains 1d6 + 2 1st-level spells, 1d4 + 2 2nd-level spells, 1d3 + 1 3rd-level spells, 1d3 4th-level spells, and a 5th-level spell.

Jingle Grells (4): HD 5; **HP** 37, 34, 33x2; **AC** 4[15]; **Atk** 10 tentacles (1d3 + paralysis), bite (1d6); **Move** 12 (flying); **Save** 12; **AL** N; **CL/XP** 9/1100; **Special:** hypnotic bells (target compelled to approach grell, save avoids, grell gets +5 bonus to hit hypnotized creatures), immune to lightning, paralysis (1d3 rounds with hit, save avoids). (**Appendix A: New Monsters**)

Room 15: Storage

Life-sized wooden dolls fill this large chamber. None of the wooden dolls is painted or decorated; instead, they either have a light pine varnish or a darker oak, pecan, or maple stain. Some of the wooden dolls are more than six feet tall, while others are only three feet tall. Some are thin and svelte, while others are broad and heavy. None of the dolls appears to have a definitive gender, but some seem vaguely masculine, some appear more feminine, and a few are genderless. This room is so full of wooden dolls that it is impossible to move through it without pushing past and brushing up against two or more dolls with every step taken.

The wooden dolls are the remains of adventurers who attempted to plunder Orcus' Claws' Candy Crypt. The unfortunate adventurers were transformed into wooden dolls by the bite of a creature known as a pheasatrice. A secret coop of **6 pheasatrices** is hidden in the southwest corner of the room. Once characters start moving through the room, the sound of the wooden dolls knocking against each other alerts the creatures that prey has entered their lair.

The Puzzle: The east corridor leads to the office (**Room 16**), but a portcullis blocks the corridor. A manual wheel to lift the portcullis is in **Room 16**, but it cannot be seen or operated by anyone inside **Room 15**. Instead, the storage room has a magical puzzle lock that can raise the portcullis. The east corridor is gothic in design, with a peaked arch that is 12 feet high at the summit. Unique clay tiles outline the arch. The tile at the peak of the arch is embossed with a star-shaped ridge, and all the tiles that outline the rest of the archway have a gutter that flows down to a pair of small holes in the floor. Any liquid poured onto the star-embossed tile at the peak splits into two channels and flows down either side of the archway, where it eventually drains into the holes on the floor. Closer inspection of the star-embossed tile reveals the ridge has an egg-shaped background. The enchanted portcullis is impervious to magical and physical harm and cannot be lifted.

The Solution: The characters need to smash a pheasatrice egg against the star-embossed tile at the peak of the archway. The bloodied yolk then oozes down both sets of guttered tiles on either side of the archway and drains into the holes on the floor. Throwing an egg at the star-embossed tile requires a successful ranged attack against AC 0[19]. One character could also lift another onto their shoulders to smash the egg against the tile by hand, but both characters suffer a –2 AC penalty. When the egg cracks and the yolk spills down the gutters, each tile illuminates in a golden yellow light. Manually cracking two eggs into the drains at the base of the arch does not raise the portcullis.

Characters suffer a –2 penalty to attacks made in the room because of the multitude of wooden dolls. The wall concealing the pheasatrices' coop has gaps in the bricks that the creatures can move through. Knocking down the wall of loosely stacked bricks exposes the coop. The six pheasatrices typically leave the coop one at a time to attack intruders, but if the wall concealing their coop is knocked down, all remaining pheasatrices attack. The coop contains 3d6 pheasatrice eggs, each worth 250 gp to an alchemist.

Pheasatrices (6): HD 5; **HP** 34, 32, 30, 28, 27, 26; **AC** 6[13]; **Atk** bite (1d6 + petrify); **Move** 6/18 (flying); **Save** 12; **AL** N; **CL/XP** 8/800; **Special:** petrify (bite turns target to wood, save avoids). (**Appendix A: New Monsters**)

Room 16: The Office

The large bloodstained stone altar in the center of the room is being used as a desk. Four torches on eight-foot-tall iron rods are positioned near the corners of the desk. A dour-looking human wearing expensive robes sits at the desk and scratches at a scroll with a quill in his hand.

A wheel that operates the portcullis in the corridor leading to the storage area (**Room 15**) is in the northwest corner of the room. The gentleman introduces himself as Sir Ramasin Kalam, a demi-knight, scribe, and oracle tasked with managing the daily operations of the Candy Crypt. In truth, Kalam is a **rakshasa**. Kalam does not want to be disturbed. He refuses to help anyone who calls out to him from the portcullis, and he becomes terribly angry if anyone enters his room. While in his human guise, Kalam appears to have a great tiger tattoo across his chest and back. When he transforms into his true rakshasa form, the tattoo ripples, envelops his whole body, and he manifests as a ferocious tiger-man.

If Kalam is destroyed and the desk searched, the characters discover a scroll titled, *Opening the Way through Gorgon Major* (see **sidebox**). The scroll details the ritual required to open a gateway for Nohell Claws to return to this plane of existence, as well as a separate ritual for closing and sealing the gate. The scroll can be read by magic-users, clerics, druids, paladins, or elves. The Gorgon Major gate can be closed only by using this scroll. In addition to the scroll, the adventurers discover a *luckstone* (+2 bonus to saves and attacks) being used as a paperweight, a leather-bound book written by Sir Ramasin Kalam titled, *Eye of the Tiger: A Memoir* (it is a *manual of intelligence*), a *crystal ball* on a small bronze tripod, and a small chest with 3d10 + 20 gp and 2d12 small gems worth 30 gp each.

Sir Ramasin Kalam (Rakshasa): HD 7; **HP** 45; **AC** –4[23]; **Atk** scimitar (1d8+3), or 2 claws (1d3), bite (1d6); **Move** 15; **Save** 9; **AL** C; **CL/XP** 12/2,000; **Special:** +1 or better magic weapons to hit, illusionary appearance (nonthreatening appearance), special magic resistance (affected only by 8th- or 9th-level spells), spells, vulnerability (blessed crossbow bolts strike as +3 missile weapon). (***Monstrosities*** 381)

Spells: 1st—*cure light wounds*, *magic missile* (x3); 2nd—*mirror image*, *web*; 3rd—*fly*.

Equipment: *+3 scimitar* (*Hawkeye*) (see **Appendix B: New Magic Items**).

Opening the Way through Gorgon Major (Scroll)

This scroll contains the ritual needed to open or close the Gorgon Major gate. For the characters to use the scroll to close the gate, one character must read from the scroll and accumulate five successful saving throws before Mr. Giggles achieves five successful saves. In the event of a tie, Mr. Giggles wins. If the Gorgon Major gate is successfully opened, Nohell Claws steps through. See the Observatory (**Room 19**) for more details.

Area 17: The Void

The hallway narrows to only five feet wide for a distance of 10 feet. The cobblestone floor is unchanged in the short stretch of hallway, but the walls and ceiling are dramatically different. The walls and ceiling are black as pitch, and they seem to rapidly vibrate with a subsonic hum. Your hairs rise into gooseflesh as you draw closer. Your gut tells you that something is very wrong with the walls in that part of the hallway, something otherworldly.

The disturbing portion of the hallway is a wound, an open scar to a plane of chaos that hungers for life and that literally attempts to grab anyone who passes through the narrow corridor. As the characters move through the narrow corridor, 1d3 + 1 arms and tentacles of various sizes and shapes reach from the void to grab each of them. The appendages attack as a 5HD creature and hold a character with a successful hit. To wriggle free, a character must succeed on a saving throw with a penalty equal to the number of arms holding him or her (so if two arms strike, the save is made with a –2 penalty). If the save fails, the character is pulled halfway into the void. Characters can make one more saving throw (with the same penalty as before) to pull themselves back into the hallway. Up to three companions can assist in this effort, with each granting a +1 bonus to the new saving throw. Otherwise, the character is pulled through the wall and lost forever. A character that escapes back into the hallway must still make a saving throw (with the appropriate penalty) to wriggle free.

Room 18: The Throne Room

This room is enormous, with a ceiling that is 30 feet high. Three huge 15-foot-diameter chandeliers are evenly spaced down the length of the room, each casting a sickly yellow light into every corner of the room. A huge line of seemingly mindless people is queued in a zig-zag pattern that runs the full length of the room. The procession begins in a niche in the northwest corner of the room, where an open dimensional door allows the people to slowly shuffle through. The line ends at the southern end of the room, where jolly ol' Orcus' Claws sits upon a throne of bones. The bones are festively painted red, white, and green.

The belly laugh of **Orcus' Claws** is more of a "Har-har-harrr" than a "Ho-ho-hooo!" Claws has delegated the task of summoning his beloved Nohell Claws to his able astrologer, Mr. Giggles, which allows Claws the time to convert more damned souls into his legion of the Naughty. It takes three combat rounds of Claws whispering into the ear of a soulless wretch to transform it into one of the Naughty. Claws cannot belly laugh and whisper to the soulless at the same time. When the characters enter the room, Claws has already created four of the Naughty. **Six Crueltide elves** and **10 brownie bites** manage the line of soulless wretches. The wretches only have 1 hit point each and AC 9[10]. They feel no pain and take no interest in anything or anyone around them.

The portal from which the procession of soulless wretches emerge leads to a level deep within the Abyss. If the characters choose to escape the Candy Crypt by traveling to the Abyss, then you should close the curtains on this adventure and prepare something for them to explore in the Abyss.

If he senses his end is near, Orcus' Claws teleports away in a cloud of fire and brimstone to a secret lair deep within the Abyss to recuperate. If his throne is searched, the characters discover a large chest hidden in a secret compartment under the seat. The chest is trapped and releases a cloud of poisonous gas in a 10-foot radius unless the trap is successfully disarmed. The gas causes a victim's flesh to violently blister and pop for 3d8 points of damage unless a saving throw is made for half damage.

The chest contains 4d6 x 50 gp, 3d12 large gems worth 125 gp each, a black silk sack containing a *robe of eyes*, a pan flute made from human bones (*pipes of the sewers*), and a stone earth elemental figurine designed to hold incense sticks (a *stone of controlling earth elementals*).

Orcus' Claws: HD: 10; **HP** 70; **AC** −2[21]; **Atk** 2 fists (2d6), tail sting (1d6 + cold poison); **Move** 12/12 (flying); **Save** 5; **AL** C; **CL/XP** 12/2000; **Special:** +1 or better magic weapons to hit, belly laugh (+1 to hit and saving throws for minions), cold poison (save or trapped in block of ice, roll below strength on 4d6 to escape), magic resistance (35%). **(Appendix A: New Monsters)**

Brownie Bites (10): HD 1; **HP** 6x10; **AC** −1[20]; **Atk** bite (1d4); **Move** 20 (flying); **Save** 17; **AL** N; **CL/XP** 3/60; **Special:** none. **(Appendix A: New Monsters)**

Crueltide Elves (6): HD 2; **HP** 13, 10x3, 9x2; **AC** 7[12]; **Atk** short sword (1d6) or deadly contraption; **Move** 12; **Save** 16; **AL** C; **CL/XP** 3/60; **Special:** Crueltide contraptions (deadly toys), darkvision (60ft). **(Appendix A: New Monsters)**
Equipment: short sword, *bag of limited holding*.

The Naughty (4): HD 2; **HP** 13, 11, 9, 8; **AC** 3[16]; **Atk** weapon (1d6) or stinger (1d3 + paralysis); **Move** 12; **Save** 16; **AL** C; **CL/XP** 3/60; **Special:** paralysis (1d4 turns, save with −2 penalty avoids). **(Appendix A: New Monsters)**

Room 19: The Observatory

This large room has a domed ceiling enchanted to display a dark sky full of stars in motion. The stars make up the amazing constellation of Gorgon Major as it rises above a vortex gateway of swirling energy on the east wall. The silhouette of a bat-winged woman with long flowing hair is fighting her way through the vortex to enter this chamber. Standing before the vortex is a dwarf with fluffy pink hair and a beard, and he wears a robe covered in gumdrops. The dwarf is raising his arms toward the vortex and chanting at the portal. As you enter the room, a host of demonic minions in the room turn to face you!

A lot is happening in this room, so take careful note of all the moving parts. The four main aspects of this room are:

1) Mr. Giggles needs five successful saving throws to finish opening the Gorgon Major gate;

2) The characters need five successful saving throws to permanently close the Gorgon Major gate;

3) The horde of demonic minions is ready to battle the characters;

4) Nohell Claws might enter the room and engage the characters.

Mr. Giggles is not a true dwarf; he is actually a dwarf-like demon known as a faerhle. Each round, if Mr. Giggles does not take any damage before he acts (and thus maintains his concentration), he may attempt one saving throw towards opening the Gorgon Major gate.

A character reading from the *Opening the Way through Gorgon Major* scroll (see sidebox in the Office [**Room 16**]) who does not take damage before he or she acts in a round may also attempt a saving throw to close the Gorgon Major gate.

The demonic minions in the room are arauks and, as luck would have it, there are the same number of arauks as there are characters. Each arauk carries four kukri short swords.

Nohell Claws is a unique succubus demon. She is ample and curvy and the bride of Orcus' Claws who has been trapped in a realm beyond the stars for a millennium. Finally, the stars are right, and a way can be opened for her return. Nohell can sense the characters fighting against her return, and it enrages her. If she successfully escapes her exile, she exacts her wrath upon the characters.

Mr. Giggles, Faerhle Demon: HD 9; **HP** 60; **AC** 1[18]; **Atk** flail (1d8), beard (entangle); **Move** 12; **Save** 6; **AL** C; **CL/XP** 10/1400; **Special:** +1 or better magic weapons to hit, entangle (30ft radius, ranged attack, as *web* spell), immune to mind-altering spells, magic resistance (15%). **(Appendix A: New Monsters)**

Arauk Demons (equal to the number of characters): HD 8; **HP** 40 each; **AC** 0[19]; **Atk** 4 kukri (1d6); **Move** 12 (fly 12); **Save** 8; **AL** C; **CL/XP** 11/1700; **Special:** breath weapon (10ft-diameter fiery cloud, 1d6 damage), resistances (cold, electricity, fire, and poison) (50%), spell-like abilities. **(Monstrosities 88)**
Spell-like abilities: at will—*darkness* (5ft radius), *detect invisibility*, *fear*, *telekinesis* (100 lbs.); 1/day—*teleport*.

Nohell Claws, Succubus Demon: HD 8; **HP** 60; **AC** 9[10]; **Atk** 2 scratches (1d3); **Move** 12 (fly 18); **Save** 8; **AL** C; **CL/XP** 11/1700; **Special:** +1 or better magic weapons to hit, level drain (drain 1 level with kiss), magic resistance (70%), shapechange (at will), spell-like abilities, summon demons (40% chance, baalroch or nalfeshnee). **(Swords & Wizardry Complete Rulebook)**
Spell-like abilities: at will—*charm person, clairaudience, darkness 15ft radius, ESP, suggestion.*

Final Conflict?

Ideally, the conflict in the Observatory (**Room 19**) is the conclusion of this dungeon delve. Assuming the characters defeat Mr. Giggles and prevent Nohell Claws from entering this realm (or if she does enter and they defeat her), then the looming threat in this adventure has been resolved and you can "fade to black" with the players having had a satisfying end to the game. However, it is also likely that the characters did not fully explore the Candy Crypt before the finale occurred. So what should you do if your players want to continue exploring this sugar and spice hellscape?

The denizens of the Candy Crypt are anxiously awaiting the coming of Nohell Claws, and they sense if she is repelled or defeated. In that case, if the orchestra is still under the thumb of the choir of erinyes demons, then the music changes in pitch and tone to something more somber and dire. This new melody of melancholy grants all creatures native to the Candy Crypt a +2 bonus to hit and damage. The foul creatures that dwell within the Candy Crypt have no reason to retreat or flee from the invasive adventurers.

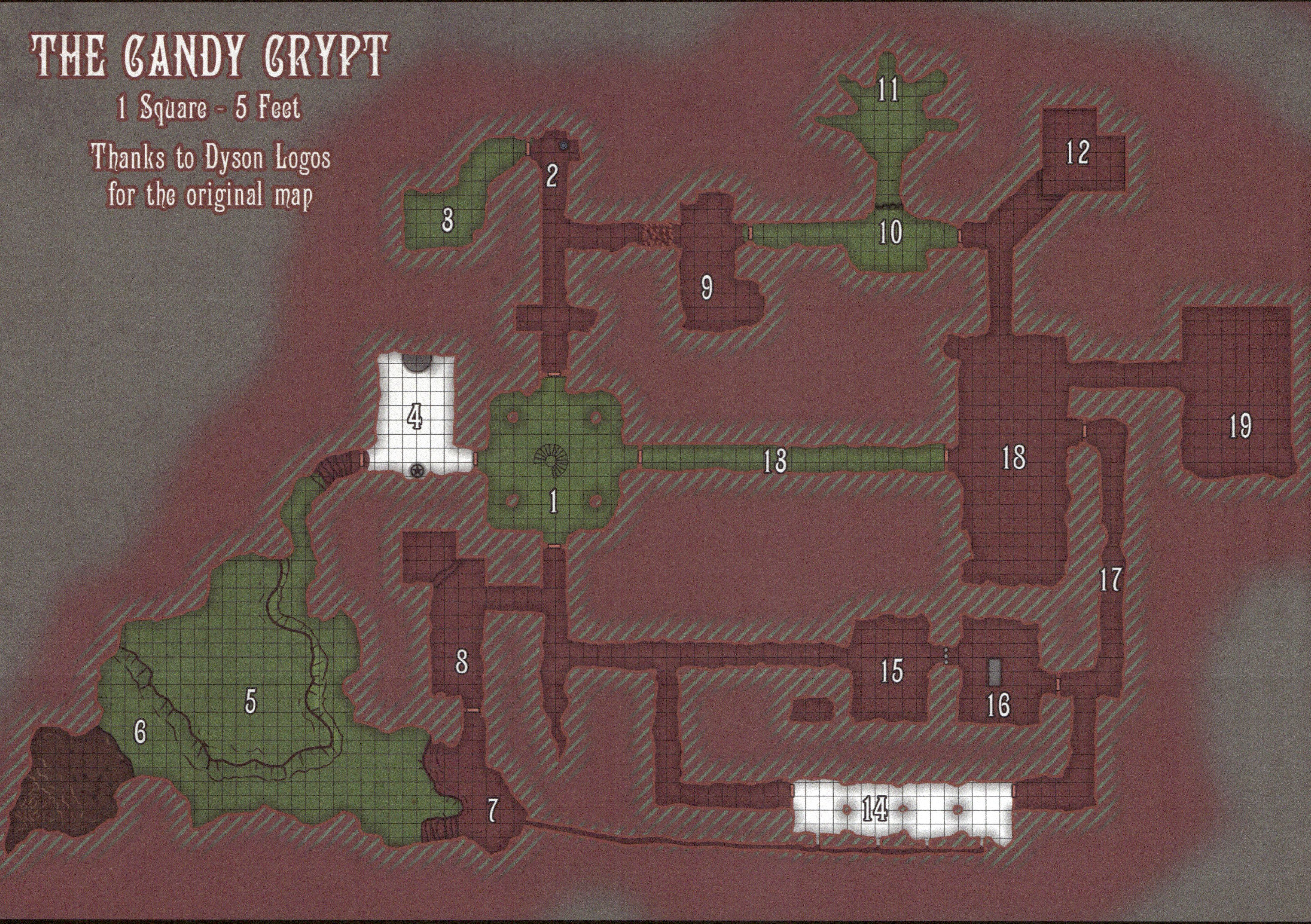

THE CANDY CRYPT
1 Square - 5 Feet
Thanks to Dyson Logos
for the original map

The following new monsters are found in this merry adventure:

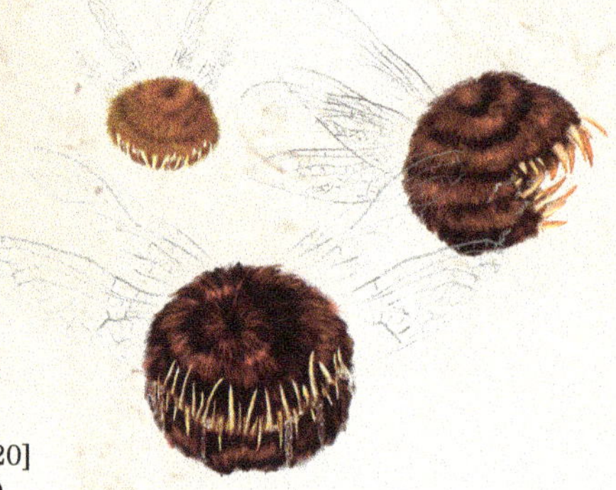

Brownie Bites

Hit Dice: 1
Armor Class: −1[20]
Attacks: bite (1d4)
Saving Throw: 17
Special: None
Move: 20 (flying)
Alignment: Neutral
Challenge Level/XP: 3/60

Brownie bites are eyeless, fist-size balls of fur. Half their body is a mouth filled with rows of razor-sharp teeth. They have a pair of dragonfly-like wings that allow them to flit and buzz around at amazing speeds. They are incredibly difficult to hit due to their uncanny speed.

Brownie Bites: HD 1; AC −1[20]; **Atk** bite (1d4); **Move** 20 (flying); **Save** 17; **AL** N; **CL/XP** 3/60; **Special:** none.

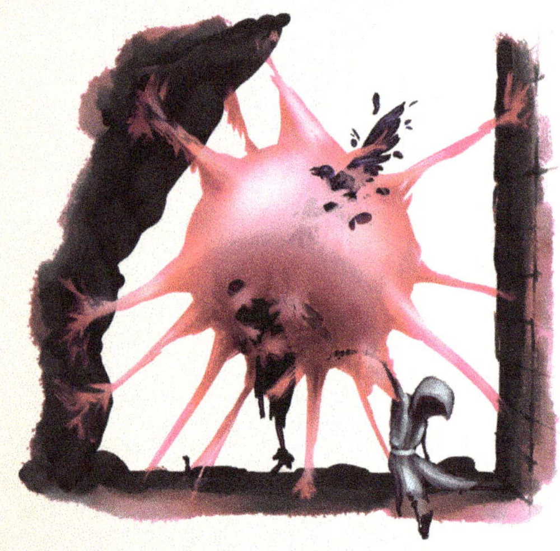

Bubblegum Sphere

Hit Dice: 5
Armor Class: 8[11]
Attacks: strike (paralysis + glue)
Saving Throw: 12
Special: Digest, glue, immune to lightning and fire, paralysis
Move: 6 (flying)
Alignment: Neutral
Challenge Level/XP: 6/400

Bubblegum spheres are a spherical mass of gelatinous polymer, with an outer surface that is gummy and sticky. Contrary to popular belief, they are not hollow on the inside. With a successful melee attack, the bubblegum sphere touches a target. On a failed saving throw, that victim sticks to the sphere and is paralyzed. Once stuck, the bubblegum sphere absorbs and digests the victim, automatically inflicting digestion damage each round. Victims can be pulled free from the sphere by their companions. Any melee weapon that strikes the sphere becomes stuck if the attacker fails a saving throw.

Bubblegum Sphere: HD 5; AC 8[11]; **Atk** strike (paralysis + glue); **Move** 6 (flying); **Save** 12; **AL** N; **CL/XP** 6/400; **Special:** digest (2d4 damage per round to stuck targets), glue (target stuck after successful strike, save avoids), immune to lightning and fire, paralysis (save avoids).

Candied Golem

Hit Dice: 8
Armor Class: 8[11]
Attacks: 2 fists (2d8)
Saving Throw: 8
Special: Immune to most spells, immune to slashing and piercing weapons
Move: 12
Alignment: Neutral
Challenge Level/XP: 13/2,300

Candied golems have a hard candy shell over a soft fleshy center. Slashing and piercing weapons do minimal damage, but blunt weapons inflict their normal damage. Candied golems are immune to all but fire-based spells. If destroyed, a candied golem breaks open and its fleshy core oozes onto the floor.

Candied Golem: HD 8; HP 45; AC 7[12]; **Atk** 2 fists (2d8); **Move** 12; **Save** 8; **AL** N; **CL/XP** 13/2300; **Special:** immune to most spells (affected only by fire-based spells), immune to slashing and piercing weapons.

CHOCOLATE PUDDING

Hit Dice: 6
Armor Class: 8[11]
Attacks: smother (2d6)
Saving Throw: 11
Special: +1 or better magic weapons to hit, vulnerable to water
Move: 6
Alignment: Neutral
Challenge Level/XP: 7/600

Chocolate puddings are amorphous blobs of milk chocolate with large chunks of dark fudge floating throughout its mass. When it attacks, the pudding attempts to smother and drown its victim in chocolate. Once enveloped, the victim can escape only by having water poured onto him. Water dilutes the chocolate, dealing 1d6 points of damage per round of contact to the creature, and allows a trapped victim to escape. The chocolate pudding automatically inflicts smothering damage on an enveloped victim. If a victim dies by smothering, the body is digested and converted into large chunks of dark fudge. Nonmagical weapons have no effect on the chocolate pudding, but magical weapons inflict normal damage on the creature.

Chocolate Pudding: HD 6; AC 8[11]; **Atk** smother (2d6); **Move** 6; **Save** 11; **AL** N; **CL/XP** 7/600; **Special:** +1 or better magic weapons to hit, vulnerable to water (1d6 damage per round).

CRUELTIDE ELF

Hit Dice: 2
Armor Class: 7[12]
Attacks: weapon (1d6) or deadly contraption (see below)
Saving Throw: 16
Special: Crueltide contraption, darkvision
Move: 12
Alignment: Chaotic
Challenge Level/XP: 3/60

These strange goblinoid creatures were corrupted by Orcus' Claws' dark influences. They have wicked, inhuman grins filled with needle-like teeth, sallow orange skin, and unusually pointed ears. They wield weapons of crudely crafted iron that leave jagged and painful wounds, and they laugh and cackle as they fight. They wear ridiculous red-and-green motley outfits that they accentuate with curled-toe shoes and jingle bells.

Despite their name, Crueltide elves are not true elves. They simply call themselves such for their own twisted enjoyment. They are instead a strange sub-race of goblins, though they are quite skilled at mechanical engineering — especially when it comes to designing deadly toys. Crueltide elves frequently carry *bags of limited holding* (see **Appendix B: New Magic Items**) that hold 1d2 Crueltide contraptions — wicked and deadly toys — that they gleefully use in battle. The table below list various contraptions, but feel free to invent more devices for the wicked little creatures to use.

1d6	Contraption
1	**Cracker-Jax:** This toy consists of a ball and 2d4 caltrops. The small red rubber ball has two stark-white stars painted on the sides and is packed with explosive powder and metal shards. A small fuse sticks out of the ball. With a successful melee attack, the Crueltide elf lights the fuse and bounces the ball at a target up to 20 feet away. The ball explodes and inflicts 1d8 points of damage to anyone within 10 feet of the blast. The caltrops are dropped on the floor to protect the elf; any creature that comes within arm's reach of the elf must make a saving throw to avoid the caltrops. On a failed save, the creature takes 1d4 points of damage.
2	**Dolly Doo-Whip:** This cute doll has long sweeping hair. The Crueltide elf grabs the doll and begins to swing her around vigorously. With each swing, the doll's hair gets longer, longer, and longer. One combat round after drawing the doll, the doll's hair turns into a long whip with barbs on the end. With a successful melee attack, the hair-whip inflicts 1d6 + 1 points of damage.
3	**Rolling Blades:** These are a pair of deadly wheeled shoes covered in razor-sharp blades. The Crueltide elf gains a free melee attack while the elf is moving during the combat round. With a successful melee attack, the bladed shoes slash at the victim as the elf skates past, inflicting 1d4 points of damage. The elf's movement must take him within melee attack range of the intended target.
4	**Stick Horse:** This toy is a three-foot-long stick with a jet-black horse head on one end. The toy horse head is that of a nightmare, with bright red eyes and a mane. Up to three times per day, the elf can quickly double-tap the stick on the floor to cause the nightmare stick horse to shoot fire from its eyes. A successful missile attack is required to hit a target up to 20 feet away. The fire inflicts 4d6 points of damage, or half as much with a successful saving throw.
5	**Tribal Drum:** This musical instrument stands two feet tall and has a 10-inch-diameter drumhead. The elf tucks the drum under one arm and begins striking it with the other hand. The drum produces a sound that is hypnotic to all creatures other than demons and demonic spawn (like the Crueltide elves). Creatures who hear the enchanted music are affected as if by a *charm person* spell.
6	**Voodoo Dolly:** This soft cloth dolly has nondescript features and a clay head. If the Crueltide elf makes a successful melee attack against an injured foe, the dolly soaks up some of the foe's blood. The dolly's clay head then transforms into the likeness of the foe whose blood it absorbed, cementing the bond between the voodoo dolly and the target. Three times per day, the Crueltide elf can stab the voodoo dolly with a needle to inflict 1d6 points of damage to the bonded victim. The elf can instead hold the voodoo dolly over an open flame to immediately inflict 3d8 points of damage to the bonded target (but this also destroys the dolly). A successful saving throw reduces any damage inflicted by the voodoo dolly by half.

Crueltide Elves: HD 2; AC 7[12]; **Atk** weapon (1d6) or deadly contraption; **Move** 12; **Save** 16; **AL** C; **CL/XP** 3/60; **Special:** Crueltide contraptions (deadly toys), darkvision (60ft).

Demon, Faerhle (First-Category Demon)

Hit Dice: 9
Armor Class: 1[18]
Attacks: weapon (by weapon), beard (entangle)
Saving Throw: 6
Special: +1 or better magic weapon to hit, entangle, immune to mind-altering spells, magic resistance (15%)
Move: 12
Alignment: Chaotic
Challenge Level/XP: 10/1,400

Faerhle are unique first-category demons that bear a strong resemblance to dwarves. Faerhles have three fingers on each hand, and their large beards are made up of a fluffy, sticky substance that grows in a variety of bright colors. A faerhle's beard is very much like cotton candy. With a successful ranged attack, a faerhle can shoot a glob of its beard at a target up to 30 feet away to entangle them (as per a *web* spell). Many faerhle arm themselves with flails or other heavy two-handed weapons. They are immune to mind-altering spells and have a general resistance to magic (15%).

Faerhle Demon: HD 9; AC 1[18]; Atk flail (1d8), beard (entangle); **Move** 12; Save 6; AL C; **CL/XP** 10/1400; **Special:** +1 or better magic weapons to hit, entangle (30ft radius, ranged attack, as *web* spell), immune to mind-altering spells, magic resistance (15%).

Demon, Kringkuk (First-Category Demon)

Hit Dice: 6
Armor Class: 1[18]
Attacks: 2 talons (1d6), bite (1d8 + poison venom)
Saving Throw: 11
Special: immune to cold, poison venom, resistances (electricity, fire, poison), webbing
Move: 6/16 (flying)
Alignment: Chaotic
Challenge Level/XP: 10/1,400

Kringkuks are a rare first-category arctic demon. They are snow white in color with an owl's torso and wings. Their large round head has six black, spider-like compound eyes and a tarantula's mandible. The demon has four pairs of insectoid legs that are covered in white fur instead of black chiton. Their two pairs of forelegs serve as the demon's arms, while the two rear pairs are the demon's legs.

Kringkuks take half damage from electricity, fire, and poison gas; they are immune to all cold attacks. Three times per day, they can cast *web* to fill a 20-foot cube. A kringkuk's bite contains a powerful venom that does 2d4 points of damage, or half as much with a successful saving throw.

Kringkuk Demon: HD 6; AC 1[18]; Atk 2 talons (1d6), bite (1d8 + poison venom); **Move** 6 (fly 16); **Save** 11; AL C; **CL/XP** 10/1,400; **Special:** immune to cold, poison venom (2d4 damage, save for half damage), resistances (electricity, fire, poison) (50%), webbing (3/day, 20ft cube, as *web* spell).

Gingersnap Man

Hit Dice: 4
Armor Class: 5[14]
Attacks: weapon (1d4)
Saving Throw: 13
Special: Immune to fire and mind control, vulnerable to water
Move: 14
Alignment: Chaotic
Challenge Level/XP: 7/600

Gingersnap men stand 2–1/2 feet tall and are only six inches thick. They emerge from the hellfire oven already decorated with icing that defines their face and clothing. When a gingersnap man dies, it bleeds icing. They are vulnerable to water, which inflicts double damage against their bodies.

Gingersnap men can be eaten but doing so could cost a creature its life. A creature that eats a gingersnap man is healed for 1d3 hit points but must make a saving throw with a bonus equal to the number of hit points recovered. On a failed save, the creature gains a candy curse:

Candy Curses

1d6	Candy Curse
1	The character's hair transforms into red and white taffy that smells like strawberries.
2	Shards of candy canes sprout from the character's shoulders, elbows, and knees.
3	Hot fudge oozes from the victim's eyes, ears, and nose, but it does not inhibit their ability to see, hear, or smell.
4	The character's flesh turns into soft cookie dough and has a warm and inviting smell. Chunks of the victim's flesh can be eaten, and the smell has an 80% chance of attracting wandering monsters.
5	The character's flesh secretes a sticky, sugary resin that makes it difficult for the victim to let go of items. The character must make a saving throw to let go of weapons, doors, tankards of mead, or anything else. A saving throw is also required to pull a weapon free if it is used to strike the character.
6	The character begins vomiting chocolate for 2d3 rounds. A character cannot take any other actions once it begins vomiting.

Candy curses can be cured with *cure serious wounds* or *remove curse*. If a creature gains four or more active candy curses at the same time, it dies from candy overload. When rolling for a new candy curse, reroll if the victim is already afflicted by that specific curse.

Gingersnap Man: HD: 4; AC 5[14]; Atk weapon (1d4); Move 14; **Save** 13; AL C; **CL/XP** 7/600; **Special:** immune to fire and mind control, vulnerable to water (200%).

Jingle Grell

Hit Dice: 5
Armor Class: 4[15]
Attacks: 10 tentacles (1d3 + paralysis), bite (1d6)
Saving Throw: 12
Special: Hypnotic bells, immune to lightning, paralysis
Move: 12 (flying)
Alignment: Neutral
Challenge Level/XP: 9/1,100

Jingle grells have 10 tentacles, each of which is decorated in silver bells that lend a rhythmic and musical quality to their movements. Anyone listening to their jingling bells must make a saving throw or be hypnotized into walking closer to the creature. The grell gets a +5 bonus to hit hypnotized creatures that willingly approach it. The tentacles paralyze creatures for 1d3 rounds that fail a saving throw.

Jingle Grell: HD 5; AC 4[15]; Atk 10 tentacles (1d3 + paralysis), bite (1d6); Move 12 (flying); Save 12; AL N; CL/XP 9/1100; **Special:** hypnotic bells (compelled to approach grell, save avoids, grell gets +5 bonus to hit hypnotized creatures), immune to lightning, paralysis (1d3 rounds with hit, save avoids).

Meka-Man

	Fighter	Wizard
Hit Dice:	4	4
Armor Class:	2[17]	2[17]
Attacks:	weapon (1d8) or fist (1d4+1)	wand (2d4) or fist (1d4+1)
Saving Throw:	13	13
Special:	None	None
Move: 12	12	
Alignment:	Neutral	Neutral
Challenge Level/XP:	6/400	6/400

Meka-men are experimental toy contraptions built by the Crueltide elves. The mechanical men come in two varieties: fighter or wizard. Fighters are armed with a sword, and the wizards with a wand. The wizard's wand shoots a chemical concoction designed to mimic the *magic missile* spell. The wizard meka-man strikes its target with a successful ranged attack.

Meka-Man Fighter: HD 4; AC 2[17]; Atk sword (1d8) or fist (1d4+1); Move 12; Save 13; AL N; CL/XP 6/400; **Special:** none.

Meka-Man Wizard: HD 4; AC 2[17]; Atk wand (2d4) or fist (1d4+1); Move 12; Save 13; AL N; CL/XP 6/400; **Special:** none.

Mistletroll

Hit Dice: 7
Armor Class: 4[15]
Attacks: 4 thorny vines (1d4 + envelop), bite (1d8)
Saving Throw: 11
Special: Envelop, regenerate, poison berries, spore breath weapon, vulnerable to fire
Move: 12
Alignment: Chaotic
Challenge Level/XP: 9/1,100

Intelligent and cruel, mistletrolls are the holiday hybrid of a plant and a fetid abomination. Orcus' Claws originally created the mistletrolls for the sole task of threatening little kids through postal letters. Like other trolls, a mistletroll regenerates 3 hit points per round. Any severed appendage fully regenerates into a new mistletroll in six hours. The rubbery mistletroll can stretch its thorn-covered vines up to 20 feet, allowing it to attack four different targets simultaneously. If it strikes a target, the creature must make a saving throw or be enveloped in the vines. The creature can also bite a target, and usually does so after pulling a vine-wrapped creature toward it.

Clusters of berries growing on the mistletroll are poisonous. Anyone who eats a berry dies in excruciating pain in 30 minutes if they fail a saving throw. On a successful saving throw, the character still takes 2d10 points of damage and feels sick (−1 penalty to hit and on saving throws for an hour).

Once per day, a mistletroll can breathe a cloud of spores in a 20-foot-long cloud. Anyone within the cloud must make a saving throw or be infected with mistletroll seeds. The seeds take root inside a creature and grow into a new mistletroll in 1d4 weeks. The new mistletroll bursts forth from the infected creature, killing it. On a successful save, the character instead takes 2d6 points of damage and coughs for 2d6 rounds (−1 to-hit penalty). Mistletrolls take double damage from fire and cannot regenerate any such damage.

Mistletroll: HD 7; AC 4[15]; Atk 4 thorny vines (1d4 + envelop), bite (1d8); Move 12; Save 11; AL C; CL/XP 9/1100; **Special:** envelop (save or entangled, Open Doors check to break free), regenerate (3 hp/round), poison berries (save or die, 2d10 damage and sick [−1 to hit and saves for 1 hour] with successful save), spore breath weapon (1/day, 20ft cloud, save or die in 1d4 weeks as new mistletroll grows in host, 2d6 damage on successful save and sick for 2d6 rounds [−1 to hit]), vulnerable to fire (200%).

Naughty

Hit Dice: 2
Armor Class: 3[16]
Attacks: weapon (1d6) or stinger (1d3 + paralysis)
Saving Throw: 16
Special: Paralysis
Move: 12
Alignment: Chaotic
Challenge Level/XP: 3/60

The Naughty were young people who fell from grace in their human lives because they never bent a knee in supplication to the Winter Spirit. Their acts of defiance earned them a place on Orcus' Claws' naughty list, and their souls were collected and transformed into the Naughty to serve the mighty Orcus' Claws.

The Naughty have mouths that are too wide and are filled with needle-like teeth. They have short stubby horns on their foreheads, cloven-hooved feet, and long whip-like tails that have a white stinger and pulsing venom sac on the tip. Victims stung by the tail must make a saving throw with a −2 penalty or be paralyzed for 1d4 turns.

The Naughty: HD 2; AC 3[16]; Atk weapon (1d6) or stinger (1d3 + paralysis); Move 12; Save 16; AL C; CL/XP 3/60; **Special:** paralysis (1d4 turns, save with −2 penalty avoids).

Orcus' Claws

Hit Dice: 10
Armor Class: −2[21]
Attacks: 2 fists (2d6), tail sting (1d6 + cold poison)
Saving Throw: 5
Special: +1 or better magic weapons to hit, belly laugh, cold poison, magic resistance
Move: 12/12 (flying)
Alignment: Chaotic
Challenge Level/XP: 12/2,000

As originally told in *How Orcus Stole Christmas!* by **Frog God Games**, this jolly aspect of the Demon Prince Orcus was crafted in the deepest pits of the Abyss by taking a single shaving from one of the Prince of the Undead's claws and freezing it in the coldest part of the Under Realms while enchanting it with vile magic. The creature that spewed forth, known as Orcus' Claws, is but a fragment of its progenitor's essence, yet it continues to grow ever stronger. Orcus' Claws is a corpulent beast standing seven feet tall and wearing a bloody mantle and stocking cap.

Orcus' Claws' creepy belly laugh emboldens his minions to attack. While they fight for his amusement, they are immune to morale checks and gain a +1 bonus to-hit and saving throws. If forced into combat, Orcus' Claws attacks three times per round, twice with his fists and once with his lightning-fast tail. Victims stung by his tail must make a saving throw or be frozen in a solid block of ice. Anyone encased in ice can escape with a successful roll below their strength on 4d6.

Orcus' Claws takes wicked delight in freezing his prey and then smashing them into pieces. If he rolls a fist attack with a natural 18–20 on a frozen creature, the target must make a saving throw or be slain as it shatters into a thousand chunks of frozen meat. A successful saving throw results in 3d6 points of damage, but the creature is freed from its icy prison.

Orcus' Claws is immune to nonmagical weapons and resists magic (35%).

Orcus' Claws: HD 10; AC −2[21]; Atk 2 fists (2d6), tail sting (1d6 + cold poison); Move 12/12 (flying); Save 5; AL C; CL/XP 12/2000; Special: +1 or better magic weapons to hit, belly laugh (+1 to hit and saving throws for minions), cold poison (save or trapped in block of ice, roll below strength on 4d6 to escape), magic resistance (35%).

Pheasatrice

Hit Dice: 5
Armor Class: 6[13]
Attacks: bite (1d6 + petrify)
Saving Throw: 12
Special: Petrify
Move: 6/18 (flying)
Alignment: Neutral
Challenge Level/XP: 8/800

A pheasatrice resembles a bat-winged pheasant with a long, feathered, serpentine tail. Its bite petrifies victims by turning them to wood unless a successful saving throw is made. The warm liver of a freshly killed pheasatrice smeared on a petrified victim returns the creature to flesh and blood, so long as the creature has been petrified for less than one turn.

Pheasatrice: HD 5; AC 6[13]; Atk bite (1d6 + petrify); Move 6/18 (flying); Save 12; AL N; CL/XP 8/800; Special: petrify (bite turns target to wood, save avoids).

Appendix B: New Magic Items

The following new magic items can be found in the adventure:

Bag of Limited Holding

This small bag can hold only four items, but each item can be as large as a human. Anything placed inside the bag is kept in a state of suspended animation and does not age or decompose. Any living thing placed into the bag instantly enters a comatose state and is immune to the needs of hunger and thirst. A living creature that is extracted from the *bag of limited holding* must make a saving throw. On a successful save, the creature takes 1d4+1 points of damage from the experience. On a failed save, the creature takes 2d6+2 points of damage and has a 50% chance of going insane. Usable by all classes.

Cruuf'xk

This *+2 onyx warhammer* contains the soul of Cruuf'xk, a demon of lies and temptations. Cruuf'xk's influence is strong; it telepathically whispers lies to the wielder. It tells the wielder that their so-called friends neither respect nor admire them. The wielder's only true friend is Cruuf'xk, for they are bonded by blood and battle. If the warhammer is used in battle, the wielder must make a saving throw with a –2 penalty. On a failed save, the wielder submits to the corrupt and morally abhorrent suggestions made by Cruuf'xk (as a *suggestion* spell) for one turn. These might include attacking friends, stealing a sacred object, or looting money from children. The warhammer's depths of depravity know no bounds.

Name	Cruuf'xk
To Hit	+2
Damage	1d4+3
Special	2/day—*cause serious wounds* (2d6+2 damage, save for half)
Weight	15 lbs.-
Value	450 gp

Frost Fang

This *+1 dagger* was forged during the Age of Darkness by a master Hyperborean blacksmith. It is enchanted with cold powers. The dagger is imbibed with an ancient Hyperborean intelligence, (intelligence 17) and can telepathically speak to anyone holding it. The dagger glows with a frosty blue light, and ice crystals form along the edge of the blade. Whoever wields *Frost Fang* is immune to natural cold damage. In addition to inflicting 1d6 points of cold damage with the blade, the dagger is also able to cast ice bolts (a variant of the *magic missile* spell) up to three times per day that do 1d6+1 points of damage. The wielder must make a successful ranged attack to inflict damage with an ice bolt.

Name	Frost Fang
To Hit	+1
Damage	1d4+1 plus 1d6 cold damage
Special	3/day—ice bolt (+1 ranged attack, as *magic missile*, 1d6+1 damage)
Weight	2 lbs.
Value	200 gp

Hawkeye

Ramasin Kalam forged this *+3 scimitar* when he completed his final quest to achieve his demi-knighthood. The curved blade was named *Hawkeye* for its ability to reflexively deflect incoming arrows and crossbow bolts.

Name	Hawkeye
To Hit	+3
Damage	1d8+3
Special	25% chance to deflect incoming arrows or crossbow bolts
Weight	2 lbs.
Value	350 gp

Ice Storm Sapphire

This large azure jewel glows with an inner white light. A magic-user can use the gem to cast *ice storm* a number of times depending on the season. Damage also varies based on the season. The wielder must make a saving throw when using the gem or take 1d6 points of damage. The gem is valued at 500 gp. Usable only by magic-users.

Season	Number of Uses	Ice Storm Damage
Winter	3	3d12 damage in 40ft cube
Spring	2	3d10 damage in 30ft cube
Summer	1	3d8 damage in 20ft cube
Autumn	2	3d10 damage in 30ft cube

ADVENTURES
WORTH
WINNING